Toys

Los juguetes

lohs hoo-*geh*-tehs

Illustrated by Clare Beaton

Ilustraciones de Clare Beaton

BARRON'S

doll

la muñeca

lah moon–*yeh*-kah

ball

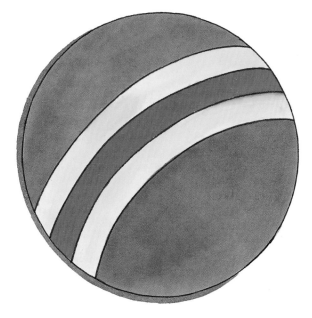

la pelota

lah peh-*loh*-tah

blocks

los cubos

lohs *koo*-bohs

car

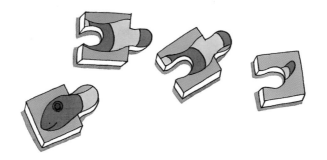

el coche

ehl *koh*–cheh

fish

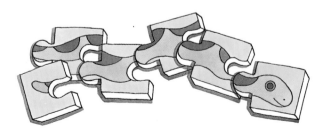

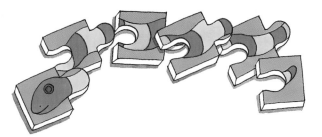

el pez

ehl pehs

drum

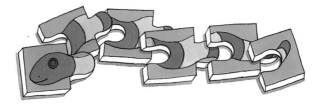

el tambor

ehl tam-*bohr*

teddy bear

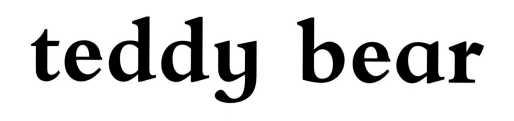

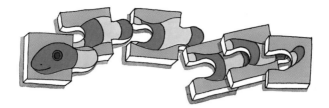

el osito

ehl oh-*see*-toh

puzzle

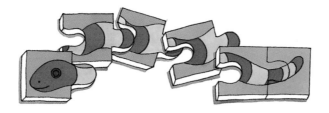

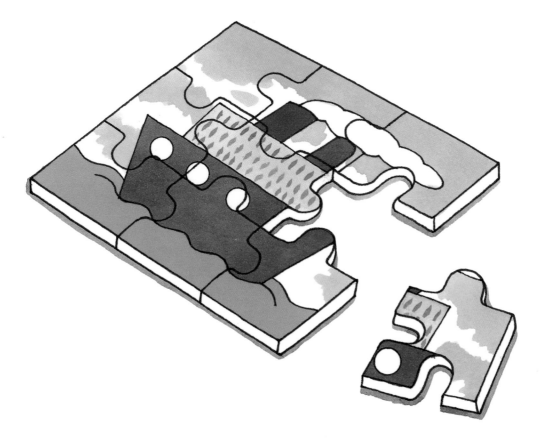

el rompecabezas

ehl rompeh-kah-*beh*-sahs

tricycle

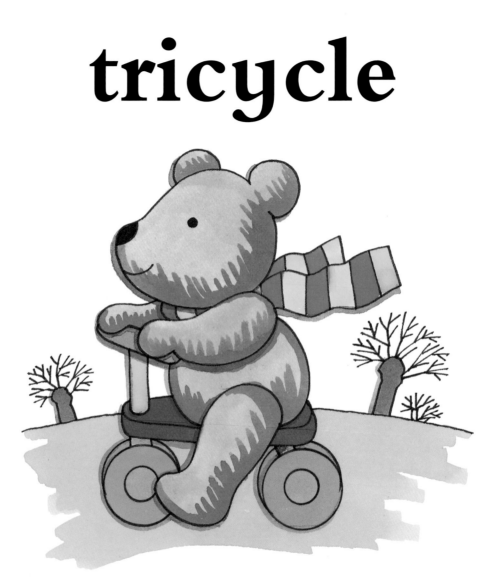

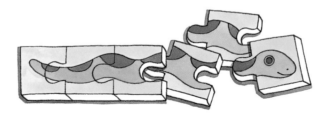

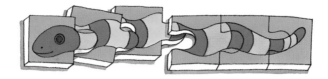

el triciclo

ehl tree-*seek*-loh

skates

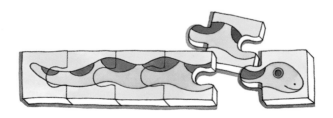

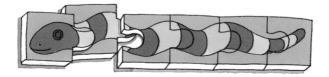

los patines

lohs pah-*tee*-nehs

crayons

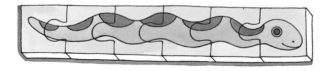

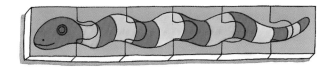

los gises de colores

lohs *hee*-sehs deh koh-*loh*-rehs

A simple guide to pronouncing the Spanish words★

- Read this guide as naturally as possible, as if it were English.
- Put stress on the letters in *italics,* e.g. ehl *koh*-cheh.

los juguetes	lohs hoo-*geh*-tehs	**toys**
la muñeca	lah moon-*yeh*-kah	**doll**
la pelota	lah peh-*loh*-tah	**ball**
los cubos	lohs *koo*-bohs	**blocks**
el coche	ehl *koh*-cheh	**car**
el pez	ehl pehs	**fish**
el tambor	ehl tam-*bohr*	**drum**
el osito	ehl oh-*see*-toh	**teddy bear**
el rompecabezas	ehl rompeh-kah-*beh*-sahs	**puzzle**
el triciclo	ehl tree-*seek*-loh	**tricycle**
los patines	lohs pah-*tee*-nehs	**skates**
los gises de colores	lohs *hee*-sehs deh koh-*loh*-rehs	**crayons**

★There are many different guides to pronunciation. Our guide attempts to balance precision with simplicity.

Text and illustrations © Copyright 2003 by B SMALL PUBLISHING, Surrey, England.
First edition for the United States, its Dependencies, Canada, and the
Philippines published in 2003 by Barron's Educational Series, Inc.
All rights reserved. No part of this book may be reproduced in any form, by photostat,
microfilm, xerography, or any other means, or incorporated into any information retrieval
system, electronic or mechanical, without the written permission of the copyright owner.
Address all inquiries to:
Barron's Educational Series, Inc., 250 Wireless Boulevard, Hauppauge, New York 11788 *(http://www.barronseduc.com)*
International Standard Book Number 0-7641-2611-3
Library of Congress Control Number 2003101096
Printed in Hong Kong   9 8 7 6 5 4 3 2 1